MW00896924

Dog Wants to Play

by **Christine McDonnell** illustrated by **Jeff Mack**

VIKING

VIKING
Published by Penguin Group
Penguin Young Readers Group, 345 Hudson Street, New York, New York 10014, U.S.A.
Penguin Group (Canada), 90 Eglinton Avenue East, Suite 700, Toronto, Ontario, Canada M4P 2Y3 (a division of Pearson Penguin Canada Inc.)
Penguin Books Ltd, 80 Strand, London WC2R 0RL, England
Penguin Ireland, 25 St Stephen's Green, Dublin 2, Ireland (a division of Penguin Books Ltd)
Penguin Group (Australia), 250 Camberwell Road, Camberwell, Victoria 3124, Australia (a division of Pearson Australia Group Pty Ltd)
Penguin Books India Pvt Ltd, 11 Community Centre, Panchsheel Park, New Delhi – 110 017, India
Penguin Group (NZ), 67 Apollo Drive, Rosedale, North Shore 0632, New Zealand (a division of Pearson New Zealand Ltd)
Penguin Books (South Africa) (Pty) Ltd, 24 Sturdee Avenue, Rosebank, Johannesburg 2196, South Africa

Penguin Books Ltd, Registered Offices: 80 Strand, London WC2R 0RL, England

First published in 2009 by Viking, a division of Penguin Young Readers Group

10 9 8 7 6 5 4 3 2 1

Text copyright © Christine McDonnell, 2009   Illustrations copyright © Jeff Mack, 2009

LIBRARY OF CONGRESS CATALOGING-IN-PUBLICATION DATA
McDonnell, Christine.
Dog wants to play / by Christine McDonnell ; Illustrated by Jeff Mack.
p. cm.
Summary: Dog is eager to have fun, but no one in the barnyard will play with him except one special friend.
ISBN 978-0-670-01126-1 (hardcover)
[1. Dogs—Fiction. 2. Domestic animals—Fiction. 3. Play—Fiction.] I. Mack, Jeff, ill. II. Title.
PZ7.M47843Dnn 2009
[E]—dc22
2009001955

Manufactured in China
Set in BB Gothic
Book design by Sam Kim

To J.D.S.
—C.M.

For Will
—J.M.

Dog wants to play.

When?

Today!

"Oh no," says the kitten.
"I might get bitten."

Poor dog.

Dog wants to play.

When?

Today!

"No, no," says the lamb.
"See how shy I am."

Poor dog.

Today!

"I don't dare," says the hare.
"I'm too easy to scare."

Poor dog.

Dog wants to play.

When?

Today!

"I'm too small," says the chick.
"Find another to pick."

Poor dog.

Dog wants to play.

When?

"No thanks," says the pig.
"Let me muck and dig."

Poor dog.

Dog wants to play.

When?

Today!

"Silly you," says the calf
and runs off with a laugh.

Poor dog.

Dog wants to play.

When?

Today!

"Yes," says the child.
"I love to be wild.

I'll play . . ."

All Day!